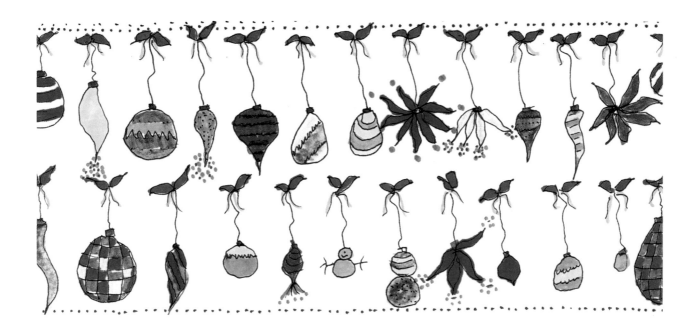

For Father Alex
and Xanthi

Paige

A Christmas Carol

By Charles Dickens
Adapted by Jesse Kornbluth
Illustrated by Paige Peterson

Gretchen B. Kimball

Patron of the arts, whose generosity
has made this book possible.

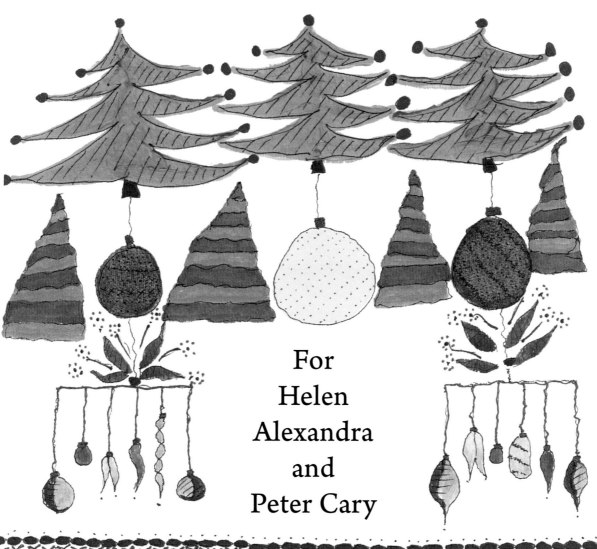

For
Helen
Alexandra
and
Peter Cary

A CHRISTMAS CAROL

A lifetime ago, I left the suburbs of Philadelphia to become a boarding student at Milton Academy, a school so different from anything I knew that it might as well have been on the moon.

Suits at dinner? Amazingly, we wore them.

Toothpaste inspection? Yes, and your shoes had to be spit-polished.

Doing your homework in a communal study hall? Ninety minutes a night.

In those days, Milton --- like many New England boarding schools --- was staunchly traditional. Teachers were addressed as "sir." There was a girls' school across the street, but we had no co-ed classes. And before the prom, we rushed to get our "dance cards" signed by our coolest friends, so our dates wouldn't think we were social outcasts.

The library was the setting for the most memorable event of my first year at Milton --- there, the night before we went home for Christmas, the headmaster read "A Christmas Carol." Arthur Bliss Perry was as Old Boston as it gets. Son of a Harvard professor who discoursed on Emerson and edited the Atlantic Monthly, he came to Milton to teach in 1921 and became headmaster in 1947. In l961, when I first encountered him, he was a figure out of time --- a tall, thin patrician, wearing three-piece suits, a school tie and eyeglasses with octagonal lenses and the thinnest of wire frames.

The Milton library was a red-brick, ivy-covered cathedral. For Mr. Perry's reading, the fireplace was lit. I believe we stood as Mr. Perry entered and took his seat in a baronial chair that had been set between the two standing lamps that were the only lights.

And then Arthur Bliss Perry became Charles Dickens.

He read without accent and without drama. He didn't play up the sentiment. He simply delivered --- as he had each December for fourteen years and would for two more --- the greatest Christmas story since the original one.

I got shivers. Maybe a tear. It was that remarkable an experience.

Decades later, I decided our daughter was ready for a version of "A Christmas Carol" not dumbed down by Disney. I didn't imagine I could equal Arthur Perry's performance, but if an audience of adolescent boys counting down the hours until their liberation could listen in rapt silence to 28,000 words, I certainly thought our tot could make it, over two or three nights, to the end.

She lasted five minutes.

Some parents, at that point, would blame her near-total boredom with Scrooge on computer games and kiddie TV and an overly permissive culture.

Not this parent.

Books change over time, and over 180 years, "A Christmas Carol" has changed more than most. The evocation of Scrooge's place of business is a slow starter. By our standards, the language is clotted and the piece is seriously overwritten --- as I was reading it, I was scanning ahead to see what I could paraphrase or cut.

And that gave me an idea. If I wanted our daughter to experience "A Christmas Carol," I needed to customize the text. My goal wasn't to rewrite Dickens, just to update the archaic language, trim the dialogue, cut the extraneous characters --- to reduce the 27,405-word book to its essence, which is the story. In the end, I did have to write a bit, but not, I hope, so you'll notice; I think of my words as minor tailoring, like sewing on a missing button or patching a rip at the knee.

The "Christmas Carol" that awaits you is half the length of the original. Like the Paige Peterson illustrations that accompany it, it means to convey the feeling of London in 1843 without the formal diction and Victorian heaviness. It pleases me when adults tell me they have read it to their delighted children and when teachers write me to report that they've read it to students who were silent and involved. I'm especially pleased that kids, starting with my daughter, can read it by themselves with pleasure, right to the end.

Jesse Kornbluth

PART 1
MARLEY'S GHOST

Marley was dead. That was a fact. His certificate of death was official. And then Scrooge signed it, which was the right thing to do, for Scrooge had been Marley's business partner for many years. And more: He had been Marley's only friend.

After Marley's death, Scrooge never painted out his name. There it stood, years later, above the warehouse door: Scrooge and Marley. Sometimes people who wandered in for the first time called Scrooge Scrooge, and sometimes Marley. He answered to both names ---- it was all the same to him.

Scrooge didn't keep the old sign out of sentiment or respect to Marley. He was just saving money. For Scrooge was the cheapest of the cheap, so tight-fisted that if the coins in his hand could talk, they would scream. His cheapness was cold and hard, and it froze him from the inside out; it shriveled his cheek, made his eyes red and his thin lips blue. He seemed to carry winter around with him.

People noticed. And they avoided him. Nobody ever stopped him in the street to say, 'My dear Scrooge, how are you? When will you come to see me?' No beggars asked him for help, no children asked him what time it was, no one ever asked him for directions.

But what did Scrooge care? Being left alone --- he liked that.

And so it was that three o'clock in the afternoon on the day before Christmas found Scrooge working away at his desk. It was cold, bleak, biting weather. He could hear the people walking past his office stamping their feet on the sidewalk to warm them.

Scrooge's clerk worked in the next office. Scrooge kept the door open so he could keep his eye upon this clerk, who sat shivering as he copied letters. It gave Scrooge pleasure to see the man wrap himself in his coat. And he was absolutely delighted to see the

clerk's breath become a small cloud of smoke in the chill.

The bell jangled, and in walked Scrooge's nephew. "A merry Christmas, uncle! God save you!" he cried.

"Bah!" said Scrooge. "Humbug!"

The nephew was a young man, and a handsome one. And happy --- he seemed almost to glow with the spirit of the season.

"'Christmas a humbug, uncle?" said Scrooge's nephew. "You don't mean that, I am sure."

"I do," said Scrooge. "Merry Christmas! What right have you to be merry? What reason do you have to be merry? You're poor enough."

"What right do you have you to be sour?" the nephew asked. "What reason do you have to be depressed? You're rich enough."

Scrooge had no smart response, so he just repeated, "Humbug!"

"Don't be like that, uncle," the nephew said.

"How else can I be," Scrooge snapped, "when I live in a world of fools? Merry Christmas! I wish the day didn't exist. What's Christmas but a time when people without money buy presents they can't afford? If I had my way, every idiot who goes about with 'Merry Christmas' on his lips should be boiled with his own holiday ham and buried with a stake of holly through his heart."

"Ah, but you don't have your way," his nephew said.

"In that case," Scrooge said sternly, "you keep Christmas in your own way, and let me keep it in mine.'

"'Keep it?" his nephew said, with a short laugh. "But you don't keep it."

"Let me leave it alone, then," said Scrooge. "Much good may it do you! Much good it has ever done you!"

"There are many things I thought would do me good --- and didn't," said his nephew.

"But I am sure I have always thought of Christmas as a good time; a kind, forgiving, charitable, pleasant time. It's the only time of the year men and women seem to be of the same opinion --- they open their shut-up hearts and they think of people below them as if they really were fellow-passengers on this journey from birth to the grave. And therefore, uncle, though it has never put a scrap of gold or silver in my pocket, I believe Christmas has done me good, and will do me good; and I say, God bless it!"

The clerk in the next office couldn't help himself --- he applauded.

Scrooge whirled around. "'Let me hear another sound from you," he said, "and you'll keep your Christmas by losing your job!" He turned back to his nephew. "You're quite a powerful speaker, sir --- you should think about going into Parliament."

"Don't be angry, uncle. Come! Have Christmas dinner with us tomorrow."

"I am expected elsewhere," Scrooge said.

"Where?"

"Right here."

"Working, uncle? On Christmas?"

"Good afternoon," said Scrooge.

"I am sorry, with all my heart, to find you so resolute. We have never had any quarrel, and I won't start now. So a Merry Christmas, uncle!"

"Good afternoon,"' said Scrooge.

"And a Happy New Year!"

"Good afternoon!" shouted Scrooge.

His nephew left the room without an angry word, stopping in the next office to offer the greeting of the season to the clerk, who returned them cordially.

"There's another fellow," muttered Scrooge. "My clerk, who earns almost nothing and has a wife and family, talking about a merry Christmas. Madness!'

The clerk, in letting Scrooge's nephew out, had let two other people in. They were large men, looking prosperous and pleased with themselves. They had books and papers in their hands, and bowed to Scrooge as they entered his office.

"Scrooge and Marley's, I believe," said one of the men, with a glance at his list." Have I the pleasure of addressing Mr. Scrooge, or Mr. Marley?"

"Mr. Marley died seven years ago, this very night," Scrooge said.

"We have no doubt his generosity is matched by his surviving partner," said one of the men, presenting his business card.

Generosity? What a silly man. Scrooge and Marley had indeed been two kindred spirits --- equally mean-spirited and hard-hearted. So Scrooge frowned, and shook his head, and handed the business card back.

"In this festive season, Mr. Scrooge," the gentleman said, "many people like to help the poor, who suffer greatly at the present time. Many thousands need common necessaries; hundreds of thousands are in want of common comforts."

"Are there no prisons?" asked Scrooge.

"Plenty of prisons."

"And workhouses for those who can't pay their bills?"

"They are. And busy, too."

"I'm very glad to hear it," Scrooge said.

"So," the gentleman said, "how much would you like to give?"

"Nothing!" Scrooge replied.

"You wish to be anonymous?"

"I wish to be left alone," said Scrooge. "Since you ask me what I wish, gentlemen, that is my answer. I don't make merry myself at Christmas and I can't afford to make idle people merry."

"But these people are badly off. Some are ill. Some may die. It's our business to help them."

"It's not my business," Scrooge replied. "It's enough for a man to understand his own business, and not to interfere with other people's. Mine occupies me constantly. Good afternoon, gentlemen!"

They saw that it would be useless to pursue their point, so the gentlemen withdrew. Scrooge resumed his labors with an improved opinion of himself.

Meanwhile the fog and darkness thickened. The ancient tower of a church became invisible; it struck the hours and quarters in the clouds. The cold became intense. In the main street, the brightness of the shops made pale faces glow as they passed. Butcher shops became a glorious pageant of pheasant and duck and goose, so it was next to impossible to believe that anyone anywhere had to think about such dull realities as bargains and sales. And then it turned foggier and colder.

It was brutally cold when Scrooge rose from his desk to close the office for the day. The clerk took this moment to enter.

"Sir?" the clerk said.

Scrooge knew what was coming.

"You'll want all day tomorrow, I suppose?" said Scrooge.

"If it's convenient, sir."

"It's not convenient," said Scrooge, "and it's not fair. If I was to hold back some of your salary for it, I bet you'd think yourself badly treated."

The clerk smiled faintly.

"And yet," said Scrooge, "you don't think me badly treated, when I pay a day's wages for no work."

The clerk observed that it was only once a year.

"A poor excuse for picking a man's pocket every twenty-fifth of December!" said Scrooge, buttoning his coat to the chin. "But I suppose you must have the whole day. Be here all the earlier next morning."

The clerk promised that he would, and Scrooge walked out with a growl. The office was closed in a twinkling, and the clerk hurried home to play with his children.

Scrooge had dinner alone in a dull, badly lit restaurant. He read the newspapers, then went home to bed --- in Marley's old apartment, as it happened. It was a gloomy suite of rooms, in a gloomy building. And lonely, for nobody lived in it but Scrooge; the other rooms had been rented out as offices.

There was nothing at all particular about the knocker on the door, except that it was very large. And it is fair to say that Scrooge very rarely thought of Marley. But as he turned the key in the lock, something impossible happened --- the knocker turned into Marley's face.

It was not in deep shadow but had a dismal light about it. It was not angry or ferocious, but looked at Scrooge as Marley used to look: with ghostly spectacles turned up on its ghostly forehead. Though the eyes were wide open, they were perfectly motionless. The total effect was one of horror.

Scrooge stared at this phenomenon --- and it became a knocker again.

Was he startled? Oh, very. But he turned the key in the lock, walked in, and lighted his candle. He did pause, however, before he shut the door, and he did look cautiously behind it first, as if he half expected to see Marley's pigtail sticking out into the hall. But there was nothing on the back of the door except the screws and nuts that held the knocker on, so he said, "Pooh, pooh" and closed it with a bang.

The sound resounded through the house like thunder. But Scrooge was not a man to be frightened by echoes. He fastened the door, walked across the hall, and up the stairs.

Darkness is cheap, and Scrooge liked it. But before he shut the heavy door of his bedroom, he walked through the apartment to see that all was right.

Living room, bedroom. Both as they should be.

Nobody under the table. Nobody under the sofa. A small fire in the grate. Nobody under the bed. Nobody in the closet. Nobody in his dressing gown, which was hanging up in a suspicious attitude against the wall. Old shoes, washing-stand, and a poker for the fire.

Quite satisfied, he closed his door, and locked himself in --- double-locked himself in, which was not his custom. Thus protected against surprise, he took off his tie, put on his dressing gown and slippers and his nightcap, and sat down before the fire.

As he leaned back in his chair, his glance happened to rest upon an old, forgotten bell. Once it communicated with another suite in the building; that purpose was long forgotten. So it was with great astonishment, and with a strange, inexplicable dread, that as he looked, he saw this bell begin to swing. It swung so softly in the outset that it scarcely made a sound; but soon it rang out loudly, and so did every bell in the house.

This might have lasted half a minute, or a minute, but it seemed like an hour. The bells stopped as they had begun, together. They were followed by a clanking noise, deep down below, as if some person were dragging a heavy chain. And Scrooge remembered that he had heard ghosts in haunted houses were described as dragging chains.

The door at the building's entrance flew open with a booming sound, and then he heard the noise much louder, on the floors below; then coming up the stairs; then coming straight towards his door.

"It's humbug still!" said Scrooge. "I won't believe it."

Without a pause, a ghost came through the heavy door.

It had the same face --- Marley in his pigtail, usual waistcoat, tights and boots. The chain he drew was clasped about his middle. It was long, and wound about him like a tail. It was made for cash-boxes and padlocks. His body was transparent. Scrooge could look through his waistcoat and see the two buttons on the back of the coat.

He could not believe what he saw. Yes, that was Marley standing before him. And he felt the chill from his death-cold eyes. But he was still incredulous, and fought against his senses.

"What do you want with me?" Scrooge asked.

"Much." Marley's voice, no doubt about it.

"Who are you?"

"Ask me who I was."

"Who were you then?" said Scrooge.

"In life, I was your partner, Jacob Marley."

"Can you …can you sit down?" asked Scrooge, looking doubtfully at him.

"I can."

"Do it, then."

The ghost sat down on the opposite side of the fireplace, as if he were quite used to it.

"You don't believe in me," observed the ghost.

"I don't," said Scrooge.

"Why do you doubt your senses?"

"Because a little thing affects them. You may be an undigested bit of beef, a blot of mustard, a crumb of cheese, a fragment of an underdone potato. There's probably more of gravy about you than the grave."

Scrooge was not much in the habit of cracking jokes, nor did he feel, in his heart, by any means jolly. The truth is, he tried to be smart, as a means of fighting off his terror, for the ghost's voice disturbed him to the very marrow in his bones.

The ghost sat perfectly motionless. Then it raised a frightful cry, and shook its chain with such a dismal and appalling noise that Scrooge held on tight to his chair, to save himself from falling in a swoon. But how much greater was his horror, when the phantom unwound the bandage round its head --- and its lower jaw dropped down upon its breast.

Scrooge fell upon his knees, and clasped his hands before his face.

"Mercy!" he said. "Dreadful apparition, why do you trouble me?"

"Man of the worldly mind," the ghost replied, "do you believe in me or not?"

"I do," said Scrooge. "I must. But why do spirits walk the earth, and why do they come to me?"

"It is required of every man," the ghost said, "that the spirit within him should walk among his fellow men, and travel far and wide; and if that spirit does not do that in life, it is condemned to do so after death. It is doomed to wander through the world and witness what it cannot share but might have shared on earth and turned to happiness."

Again the ghost raised a cry, and shook its chain and wrung its shadowy hands.

"You are chained," said Scrooge, trembling. "Tell me why."

"I wear the chain I forged in life," the ghost said. "I made it link by link, and yard by yard. I created it of my own free will, and of my own free will I wore it. Is its pattern strange to you?"

Scrooge trembled more and more.

"Do you know the weight and length of the strong chair you carry?" the ghost said. It wasn't a question. "That chain was as heavy and as long as this, seven Christmas Eves ago. You have labored on it, since. It is a very weighty chain!"

Scrooge glanced about him on the floor, in the expectation of finding himself surrounded by some fifty or sixty feet of iron cable. But he could see nothing.

"'Jacob," he said, imploringly. "Old Jacob Marley, tell me more. Speak comfort to me, Jacob."

"I have none to give," the ghost replied. "Comfort comes from other regions, Ebenezer Scrooge, and is conveyed by other ministers, to other kinds of men. Nor can I tell you what I would. A very little more is all that is permitted to me. I cannot rest, I cannot stay, I cannot linger anywhere. My spirit never walked beyond our office --- in life my spirit never wandered farther than our bank. Now weary journeys lie before me."

"Seven years dead --- and traveling all the time?"

"The whole time. No rest, no peace. Incessant torture of remorse."

"You travel fast?"

"On the wings of the wind."

"You might have got over a great quantity of ground in seven years," Scrooge said.

The ghost clanked its chains.

"Yes. But no regret can make amends for a lifetime of missed opportunity. Such was I! Oh! Such was I!"

"You were always a good man of business, Jacob," Scrooge said.

"Business!" cried the ghost, wringing its hands. "Mankind was my business. The common welfare was my business --- charity, mercy and benevolence were my business. The dealings of our company were but a drop of water in the ocean of my business!"

The ghost held up its chain at arm's length, as if that were the cause of all its grief, and flung it heavily upon the ground again.

"At this time of the year," the ghost said, "I suffer most. Why did I walk through crowds of fellow-beings with my eyes turned down and never raise them to that blessed Star which led the Wise Men? Were there no poor homes to which its light would have conducted me?"

Scrooge was very dismayed to hear the ghost going on in this way, and he began to quake.

"Hear me!" cried the ghost. "My time is nearly gone"

"I will," said Scrooge. "But don't be hard upon me, Jacob!"

"Do you know," the ghost said, "that I have sat invisible beside you many and many a day?"

26

It was not an agreeable idea. Scrooge shivered, and wiped the perspiration from his brow.

"I have come here tonight to warn you: you still have a chance to escape my fate."

"You were always a good friend to me," Scrooge said. "Thank you."

"You will be haunted," the ghost said, "by three spirits."

"Is that the chance you mentioned, Jacob?" Scrooge asked, in a faltering voice.

"It is."

"I…I think I'd rather not," Scrooge said.

"Without their visits," the ghost said, "you cannot hope to avoid the path I tread. Expect the first tomorrow, when the bell tolls one o'clock."

"Couldn't I take them all at once, and have it over, Jacob?"

"Expect the second on the next night at the same hour. Expect the third upon the next night when the last stroke of twelve has ceased to vibrate. Look to see me no more; and remember, for your own sake, what has passed between us tonight."

When it had said these words, the ghost took its bandage from the table, and bound it round its head, as before. Scrooge dared to raise his eyes again and found his supernatural visitor confronting him with its chain wound over and about its arm. The ghost walked backward from him, and at every step it took, the window raised itself a little, so that when

the ghost reached it, it was wide open.

It beckoned Scrooge to approach, which he did. When they were within two paces of each other, Marley's ghost held up its hand, warning him to come no nearer. Scrooge stopped.

He stopped not so much in obedience as in surprise and fear, for on the raising of the hand, he became aware of confused noises in the air, wild sounds of anguish and regret. The ghost, after listening for a moment, joined in the mournful dirge, and floated out upon the bleak, dark night.

Scrooge followed to the window and looked out.

The air was filled with phantoms. Every one of them wore chains like Marley's ghost; a few were linked together, none was free.

Scrooge had personally known many of these phantoms when they were alive. He had been quite familiar with one old ghost, in a white vest, with a monstrous iron safe attached to its ankle, who cried piteously at being unable to assist a wretched woman with an infant. They wanted to interfere for good in human affairs --- but they had lost the power forever.

Whether these creatures faded into mist or mist enshrouded them, Scrooge couldn't tell. But they and their spirit voices faded together, and the night became as it had been when he walked home.

Scrooge closed the window and examined the door by which the ghost had entered. It was double-locked, as he had locked it with his own hands, and the bolts were undisturbed. He tried to say 'Humbug!' but stopped at the first syllable. And then, much in need of rest, he went straight to bed, and, almost immediately, fell asleep.

PART 2
THE FIRST OF THE THREE SPIRITS

Scrooge woke to the ringing of a heavy bell. To his amazement, it rang six, then seven, then eight. It stopped at twelve. Twelve! How could that be? He had gone to bed at two. The clock was wrong. An icicle must have got into the works. Twelve!

He squinted at his pocket watch. Twelve!

"It isn't possible," said Scrooge, "that I can have slept through a whole day and far into another night."

He scrambled out of bed and went to the window. All he could see was that it was dark and foggy and extremely cold, and there were no people out.

Scrooge went back to bed.

As he lay there, he thought and thought, and the more he thought the more perplexed he was --- about the strangeness of the time, but even more, about Marley's ghost. Was it a dream or not?

Then he remembered: The ghost had warned him of a visitation when the bell tolled one. He decided to lie awake until it came, but time passed slowly, and he dozed.

The church bell rang. One. Suddenly light flashed in the room and Scrooge found himself face to face with an unearthly visitor who was standing as close to him as I am now to you.

The visitor was a strange figure. It was small like a child. Its hair was white --- and yet the face didn't have a wrinkle. The arms were very long and muscular, and the hands looked uncommonly strong. Its legs and feet were bare.

At first Scrooge thought the strangest thing about the visitor was a bright clear jet of light streaming from the top of its head. But the more he looked, its strangest quality was how the figure changed --- sometimes light, sometimes dark, now seeming to have one arm and one leg, now with twenty legs, now a pair of legs without a head, now a head without a body.

"Are you the spirit whose coming was foretold to me?" Scrooge asked.

"I am," the visitor said, in a soft and gentle voice.

"Who, and what are you?"

"I am the Ghost of Christmas Past."

"Long past?"

"No," the visitor said. "Your past."

"What business brings you here?"

"Your welfare!" the ghost said. "So take heed!"

The ghost put out its hand as it spoke, and clasped Scrooge gently by the arm.

"'Rise! And walk with me!"

There would have been no point for Scrooge to plead that the weather was miserable and the hour was late and that he was only wearing his slippers, robe and nightcap --- the ghost wasn't to be resisted.

The ghost gestured for him to approach the window.

"I am mortal," Scrooge said. "I might fall."

"Take my hand."

Just as he said those words, they passed --- as if by magic --- through the wall, and stood upon an open country road, with fields on either hand. The city had entirely vanished.

The darkness and the mist had also vanished --- it was a clear, cold, winter day. "Good Heaven!" Scrooge said, clasping his hands together, as he looked about him. "I was born here. I was a boy here!"

"Your lip is trembling," the ghost said, noticing that Scrooge was silently crying. "And what is that upon your cheek?"

Scrooge muttered, with an unusual catch in his voice, that it was nothing, and begged the ghost to lead him where he would.

"You know the way," said the Spirit.

"Remember it?" cried Scrooge. "I could walk it blindfold."

"Strange to have forgotten it for so many years!" the ghost said. "Let's go on."

As they walked along the road, Scrooge recognized every gate, post and tree. A little market town appeared in the distance, with its bridge, its church, and winding river. He saw some shaggy ponies trotting towards them with boys riding them. They called to other boys in carts driven by farmers. All these boys were in great spirits, and shouted to each other, until the broad fields were filled with the joyous music of children.

"Those are only shadows of the things that used to be," said the ghost. "They aren't aware that we are here."

More people appeared. Scrooge knew and named them all. He was happy to see them, His cold eye glistened, and his heart leapt up as they went past. And he was filled with gladness when he heard them wish each other Merry Christmas as they headed off to their homes.

"The school is not quite deserted," the ghost said. "One child, neglected by his friends, is still there."

Scrooge knew that. And he sobbed.

They left the road and soon approached a mansion of dull red brick. It was a large house, but the rooms were unused, their walls were damp and mossy, and their windows were broken.

The ghost and Scrooge walked to a door at the back of the house. It opened before them, revealing a long, bare, melancholy room, made even barer by lines of desks. At one of these a lonely boy was reading near a feeble fire. Scrooge sat down and wept to see the boy --- his poor forgotten self, as he used to be.

The spirit touched him on the arm, and pointed to his younger self, intent upon his reading. Suddenly a man, in foreign clothes, stood outside the window, with an axe stuck in his belt. Behind him was a donkey laden with wood.

"Why, it's Ali Baba," Scrooge exclaimed. "It's dear old honest Ali Baba! Yes, yes, I know. One Christmas time, when that child was left here all alone, he did come, for the first time, just like that. Poor boy!"

Scrooge stopped and rubbed his eyes with his cuff.

"What is the matter?" the Spirit asked.

"Nothing," Scrooge said. "Nothing."

The ghost smiled thoughtfully, and waved its hand. "Let's see another Christmas!" he suggested.

The room became darker and dirtier. The panels shrunk, the windows cracked; fragments of plaster fell out of the ceiling --- but how all this was brought about, Scrooge knew no more than you do. He only knew that it seemed right, the way everything had happened. And there he was, alone again, when all the other boys had gone home for the jolly holidays.

The boy was not reading now, but walking up and down despairingly. Scrooge looked at the ghost, and with a mournful shaking of his head, glanced anxiously towards the door.

It opened; and a little girl, much younger than the boy, came darting in. She put her arms about his neck and kissed him.

"I have come to bring you home, dear brother!" the girl said, clapping her tiny hands, and bending down to laugh. "To bring you home, home, home!"

"Home, little Fan?"

36

"Yes!" the girl said. "Home, for good and all. Home, forever and ever. Father is so much kinder than he used to be that home's like Heaven! He spoke so gently to me one night that I asked him once more if you might come home. He said yes, you should, and he sent me in a coach to bring you. And you're to be a man, and won't ever come back here; but first, we're to be together all Christmas long, and have the merriest time in all the world."

"You are quite a woman, little Fan!" the boy exclaimed.

She clapped her hands and laughed, and tried to touch his head. She was too little, so she stood on tiptoe to embrace him. Then she began to drag him, in her childish eagerness, towards the door.

A voice in the hall cried, "Bring down Master Scrooge's box, there!" and very quickly Scrooge's trunk was tied on to the top of the carriage, and the children were telling the schoolmaster good-bye and driving toward their home.

"Always a delicate creature," the ghost said. "But she had a large heart."

"So she did."

"She had a child," the ghost said.

"One child," Scrooge noted.

"True," the ghost said. "Your nephew."

Scrooge seemed uneasy and answered briefly, "Yes."

Now they were in the busy thoroughfares of a city. Looking at the shops he could see it was Christmas time again, but it was evening, and the streets were lighted up.

The ghost stopped at a certain warehouse door, and asked Scrooge if he knew it.

"Know it?" Scrooge said. "I apprenticed here."

They went in. An old gentleman in a Welsh wig sat behind a desk so high that if he had been two inches taller he would have knocked his head against the ceiling.

40

Scrooge cried in great excitement: "Why, it's old Fezziwig! Bless his heart, it's Fezziwig alive again!"

Old Fezziwig laid down his pen, and looked up at the clock, which pointed to the hour of seven. He rubbed his hands, adjusted his vest, laughed all over himself, and called out in a comfortable, oily, rich, fat, jovial voice: "Yo ho, there! Ebenezer! Dick!"

Scrooge's former self, now grown a young man, came briskly in, accompanied by his fellow apprentice.

"That's Dick Wilkins," Scrooge said. "Bless me, yes. There he is. He was very much attached to me, was Dick. Poor Dick."

"Yo ho, my boys!" Fezziwig said. "No more work tonight. Christmas Eve, Dick. Christmas, Ebenezer! Let's have the shutters up!"

You wouldn't believe how those two fellows went at it. They charged into the street with the shutters --- one, two, three --- and had them up in their places --- four, five, six --- and barred them and pinned them --- seven, eight, nine --- and came back before you could have got to twelve, panting like race-horses.

"Hilli-ho!" cried old Fezziwig, skipping down from his desk. "Clear away, my lads, and let's have lots of room here!"

Clear away! There was nothing they wouldn't have cleared away, or couldn't have cleared away, with old Fezziwig looking on. It was done in a minute. Everything that could be moved was packed off. The floor was swept and watered, the lamps were trimmed, fuel was heaped upon the fire. The warehouse was as snug and warm and dry and bright as a ballroom.

In came a fiddler. In came Mrs. Fezziwig. In came the three Miss Fezziwigs. In came the six young followers whose hearts they broke. In came all the young men and women employed in the business. In came the housemaid, with her cousin, the baker. In came the cook, with her brother's particular friend, the milkman. In came the boy from over the way.

In they all came, one after another; some shyly, some boldly, some gracefully, some awkwardly, some pushing, some pulling; in they came. And away they went, twenty couples dancing at once, until old Fezziwig clapped his hands to stop the dancing. There were more dances, and there was cake, and there was a great piece of roast beef, and there were mince pies, and plenty to drink. But the great effect of the evening came when the fiddler struck up Mr. Fezziwig's favorite tune and the Fezziwigs danced together.

When the clock struck eleven, the party ended. Mr. and Mrs. Fezziwig took their stations, one on either side of the door, and shook hands with every person as they went out, and wished them all a Merry Christmas.

During the whole of this time, Scrooge's heart and soul were in the scene, and with his former self. He remembered everything and enjoyed everything. Only when the bright faces of his former self and Dick left the ball did he remember the ghost, and became conscious that it was looking full upon him.

"How little it takes," the ghost said, "to make these silly folks so full of gratitude."

"How little!" echoed Scrooge.

"He has spent only a few pounds --- three or four perhaps. Is that so much that he deserves this praise?'

"It isn't that," Scrooge said, speaking unconsciously like his younger self. "The happiness he gives is as great as if it cost a fortune."

He felt the ghost's glance, and stopped.

"What is the matter?" the ghost asked.

"Nothing in particular," Scrooge said. "Well, I should like to be able to say a word or two to my clerk just now. That's all."

His former self turned down the lamps, and Scrooge and the ghost again stood side by side in the open air.

"My time grows short," the ghost said. "Quick!"

This was not addressed to Scrooge, or to any one whom he could see, but it produced an immediate effect. For again Scrooge saw himself. He was older now, a man in the prime of life. His face had begun to wear the signs of care and avarice. There was an eager, greedy, restless motion in the eye, which showed the passion that had taken root --- the passion for money.

Scrooge wasn't alone now. He sat by the side of a young girl in a mourning dress. There were tears in her eyes.

"It matters little," she said, softly. "To you, very little. Another idol has displaced me; and if it can cheer and comfort you in times to come, as I would have tried to do, I have no reason to grieve."

"What idol has displaced you?" he asked.

"A golden one."

"This is the way of the world," he said. "There is nothing it pretends to hate more than the pursuit of wealth!"

She answered gently: "I have seen your nobler aspirations fall off one by one, until the passion of gain engrosses you."

"What if it has?" he retorted. "I am not changed towards you."

She shook her head.

"Well....am I?"

"Our contract was made when we were both poor and content to be so, until we could improve our worldly fortune by our hard industry. You were another man then. Now you are changed."

"I was a boy," Scrooge said impatiently.

"The way you speak tells you that you were not what you are now," she said. "I am. I release you from our contract. It's the right thing --- I can't believe any more that you would choose a poor girl. I know if you did, you would regret it. So I release you. With a full heart, for the love of the man you once were."

He was about to speak; but with her head turned from him, she continued: "The memory of what is past may give you pain. Part of me hopes for that. But it will be a very, very brief pain, and you will dismiss the memory of it. So....may you be happy in the life you have chosen!"

She left him, and they parted.

"Spirit!" said Scrooge, "show me no more! Take me home!"

"One shadow more!" the ghost said.

"No more!" Scrooge cried. "No more, I don't wish to see it. Show me no more!"

But the relentless ghost grabbed him and forced him to look at what happened next.

They were in another scene and place: a room, not very large, but comfortable. Near to the fireplace sat a beautiful young girl, so like the last girl that Scrooge believed it was the same, until he saw her --- a mother now --- sitting opposite her daughter. The noise in this room was perfectly tumultuous, for there were many children there. The place was noisy, but no one seemed to care; on the contrary, the mother and daughter laughed heartily, and enjoyed it very much. Who wouldn't want to be part of that family?

But now a knocking at the door was heard, and they all rushed to greet the father, who entered with a man struggling under the weight of Christmas toys and presents. The children grabbed the father, and tugged on him, and pounded his back, and shouted with wonder and delight as each package was set out. It seemed to take forever to clear the room of the little children and get them to bed.

And now Scrooge looked on more attentively than ever as the master of the house sat down with his eldest daughter and her mother. And he thought that a girl as graceful and as full of promise might have called him father, and been a joy to him in the winter of his life, and his sight grew very dim indeed.

"Belle," said the husband, turning to his wife with a smile, "I saw an old friend of yours this afternoon."

"Who?"

"Guess!"

44

"How can I? Oh! Wait! Was it Mr. Scrooge?"

"Mr. Scrooge it was. I passed his office window; and as it wasn't shut up, and he had a candle inside, I could see him clearly. His partner lies upon the point of death, I hear; and there he sat alone. Quite alone in the world, I do believe."

"Spirit!" Scrooge begged, "take me away from this place."

"I told you these were shadows of the things that have been," the ghost said. "They are what they are --- don't blame me!"

"Remove me!" Scrooge exclaimed. "Take me back! Haunt me no longer!"

The next thing he knew, Scrooge was conscious of being exhausted, and overcome by an irresistible drowsiness, and more, of being in his own bedroom. He barely had time to pull up the covers before he sank into a heavy sleep.

PART 3
THE SECOND OF THE THREE SPIRITS

Scrooge's snoring woke him. He immediately looked round the bed --- he didn't want to be taken by surprise. And he wondered: What curtain would this new ghost draw back?

But when the bell struck one and no ghost appeared, he was taken with a violent fit of trembling.

Five minutes, ten minutes, a quarter of an hour went by, yet nothing came. Except this: The whole time, a blaze of light streamed upon the bed --- and because it was only light and he couldn't figure out what it meant, it was more frightening than a dozen ghosts.

He got up softly and shuffled in his slippers to the door.

The moment Scrooge's hand was on the lock, a strange voice called him by his name, and ordered him to turn. He obeyed.

It was his own room. There was no doubt about that. But it had undergone a surprising transformation. The walls and ceiling were green --- it looked like a forest. Bright gleaming berries glistened from every leaf. There was holly, mistletoe and ivy. And a mighty blaze went roaring up the chimney.

Heaped up on the floor, to form a kind of throne, were turkeys, geese, poultry, suckling pigs, long wreaths of sausages, plum puddings, barrels of oysters, hot chestnuts, cherry-cheeked apples, juicy oranges, luscious pears, immense cakes and bowls of punch.

And then were was a jolly giant, holding a glowing torch, which he held high, the better to shed its light on Scrooge.

Scrooge hung his head. He was not the dogged Scrooge he had been. The ghost's eyes were clear and kind, but Scrooge did not want to look into them.

"I am the ghost of Christmas Present," the ghost said. "Look upon me!"

Scrooge did. The ghost wore a simple green robe, bordered with white fur. Its feet were bare. On its head it wore a holly wreath. Its hair was curly. Its eyes sparkled. It seemed… joyful.

"You have never seen anything like me before!" exclaimed the ghost.

"Never," Scrooge said. "Spirit, take me where you will. I went forth last night because I was forced to, and I learnt a lesson that is working now. Tonight, if you have something to teach me, let me learn from it."

"Touch my robe!"

Scrooge did as he was told.

Holly, mistletoe, red berries, ivy, turkeys, geese, game, poultry, meat, pigs, sausages, oysters, pies, puddings, fruit and punch --- all vanished instantly. So did the room, the fire, the hour of night.

Now Scrooge and the ghost stood on a city street on Christmas morning. They could see nothing very cheerful through the gloomy, dingy mist, and yet was there cheerfulness in the air. The people who were shoveling snow from their steps were happy to be doing so. Now and then a snowball would fly, and someone would shout with delight if it hit its target.

The customers in the food shops were all so hurried they tumbled against each other at the door, crashing their baskets wildly, and left their purchases upon the counter, and came running back to fetch them, all in the best spirit. And then it was time for church, and they came, flocking through the streets in their best clothes and with their most pleasant faces.

For the ghost, this was the signal to lead Scrooge to his clerk's house. There he found Mrs. Cratchit, Bob Cratchit's wife, in a faded dress. Belinda Cratchit, second of her daughters, was setting the table, while young Peter Cratchit plunged a forkful of potatoes into his mouth. And now two smaller Cratchits, boy and girl, came tearing in,

screaming that outside the baker's they had smelt the goose and just knew it was theirs.

"What has ever got your precious father?" said Mrs. Cratchit. "And your brother, Tiny Tim? And Martha wasn't as late last Christmas Day."

"Here's Martha, mother!" cried the two young Cratchits. "Hurrah! There's such a goose, Martha!"

"Why, bless your heart alive, my dear, how late you are!" said Mrs. Cratchit, kissing her a dozen times.

"We had a lot of work to finish up last night," the girl replied, "and had to clear away this morning, mother!"

"Well! Never mind so long as you are here," said Mrs. Cratchit. "Sit down before the fire, my dear."

"No, no! Father's coming," cried the two young Cratchits. "Hide, Martha, hide!"

So Martha hid herself, and in came Bob, with Tiny Tim on his shoulder. Alas for Tiny Tim, he carried a little crutch, and had his limbs supported by an iron frame.

"Where's our Martha?" cried Bob, looking round.

"Not coming," Mrs. Cratchit said.

"Not coming! Not coming on Christmas Day?"

Martha didn't like to see him disappointed, even if it was only in joke; so she came out from behind the closet door, and ran into his arms, while the two young Cratchits hustled Tiny Tim off to see the pudding as it cooked.

"And how did little Tim behave?" asked Mrs. Cratchit.

"As good as gold," said Bob, "and better. Somehow he gets thoughtful, sitting by himself so much, and thinks the strangest things you ever heard. He told me, coming home, that he hoped the people saw him in the church, because he was a cripple, and it might be pleasant to them to remember upon Christmas Day who it was that made lame beggars walk and blind men see."

Bob's voice trembled when he told them this, and trembled more when he said that Tiny Tim was growing strong and hearty.

The children went out to fetch the goose, while Mrs. Cratchit heated the gravy. Peter mashed the potatoes with incredible speed. Belinda sweetened the applesauce. Martha put out the plates. And the two young Cratchits set chairs for everybody, not forgetting themselves.

At last the dishes were set on, and grace was said. It was succeeded by a breathless pause, then Mrs. Cratchit plunged the carving knife into the goose. A murmur of delight arose all round the table, and even Tiny Tim beat on the table with the handle of his knife, and feebly cried, "Hurrah!"

There never was such a goose. Bob said he didn't believe there ever was such a goose cooked. Its tenderness and flavor, size and cheapness were the themes of universal admiration. Served with applesauce and mashed potatoes, it was a sufficient dinner for the whole family.

And then, as Belinda changed the plates, Mrs. Cratchit left the room alone to bring in the pudding. But what if it should not be done enough! What if it broke as it was being served? What if somebody got over the wall of the backyard and stole it while they were merry with the goose? All sorts of horrors were supposed.

Mrs. Cratchit entered, flushed, but smiling proudly. The pudding was like a cannon-ball, so hard and firm. "Oh, a wonderful pudding!" Bob Cratchit said, proclaiming it as the greatest success achieved by Mrs. Cratchit since their marriage. Everybody had something to say about it, but nobody said or thought it was a small pudding for a large family.

At last the dinner was all done, the cloth was cleared, the hearth swept, and the fire made up. Apples and oranges were put upon the table, and a shovel full of chestnuts on the fire. Then all the Cratchit family drew round the hearth, and Bob proposed: "A Merry Christmas to us all, my dears. God bless us!"

Which all the family echoed.

"God bless us every one!" said Tiny Tim, the last of all.

He sat very close to his father's side upon his little stool. Bob held his withered little hand in his, as if he wished to keep him by his side and dreaded that he might be taken from him.

"Spirit," said Scrooge, with an interest he had never felt before, "tell me if Tiny Tim will live."

"I see a vacant seat in the poor chimney corner, and a crutch without an owner, carefully preserved," replied the Ghost. "If these shadows remain unchanged in the future, the child will die."

"No, no," said Scrooge. "Oh, no, kind Spirit! Say he will be spared."

"If these shadows remain unchanged in the future, no one will find him here," the Ghost repeated. "What then? Didn't someone say: 'If he's likely to die, he had better do it, and decrease the surplus population.'"

Scrooge hung his head to hear his own words quoted by the ghost, and was overcome with penitence and grief. And then he heard his own name, and looked up.

"Mr. Scrooge!" Bob said. "A toast to Mr. Scrooge, the Founder of the Feast!"

"The Founder of the Feast indeed!" cried Mrs. Cratchit, reddening. "I wish I had him here. I'd give him a piece of my mind to feast upon, and I hope he'd have a good appetite for it."

"My dear, think of the children, think of Christmas Day."

"It would be Christmas Day, I am sure," she said, "on which one drinks the health of such an odious, stingy, hard, unfeeling man as Mr. Scrooge. You know he is, Robert! Nobody knows it better than you do, poor fellow!"

"My dear, it's Christmas Day."

"I'll drink his health for your sake and the day's --- not for his," said Mrs. Cratchit. "Long life to him. A merry Christmas and a happy new year! He'll be very merry and very happy, I have no doubt!"

The children drank the toast after her. It was the first of their festivities that had no heartiness. Tiny Tim drank it last of all, but he didn't care for it. Scrooge was the ogre of the family. The mention of his name cast a dark shadow on the party, which was not dispelled for full five minutes.

After it had passed away, they were ten times merrier than before, just from the relief of Scrooge being done with. Bob Cratchit told them how he had a situation in his eye for Peter, which would bring in, if obtained, quite a nice salary. The two young Cratchits laughed tremendously at the idea of Peter's being a man of business, and Peter himself looked into the fire and thought about the investments he'd make someday. Martha told them what kind of work she had to do, and how many hours she worked at a stretch, and how she meant to lie in bed tomorrow morning for a good long rest. All this time the chestnuts and the jug went round and round, and by and by they had a song about a lost child travelling in the snow from Tiny Tim.

There was nothing fancy in any of this. They were not a handsome family, they were not well dressed, their shoes were far from being waterproof. But they were happy, and grateful, and pleased with one another.

Scrooge had his eye upon them, and especially on Tiny Tim, until the last.

By this time it was getting dark, and snowing pretty heavily. As Scrooge and the ghost went along the streets, the brightness of the roaring fires in the houses was wonderful. Here the flickering of the blaze showed preparations for a cozy dinner. There all the children of the house were running out into the snow to meet their married sisters, brothers, cousins, uncles, aunts, and be the first to greet them. Here, again, were shadows on the window blind of guests assembling. And there was a group of handsome girls, all chattering at once, as they tripped lightly off to some neighbor's house.

If you had judged from the numbers of people on their way to friendly gatherings, you might have thought that no one was at home to give them welcome when they got there, instead of every house expecting company, and piling up its fires half-chimney high. Blessings on it, how the ghost enjoyed what it saw!

But now, without a word of warning from the ghost, they stood in a bleak and desert field, where masses of stone were cast about as though this was the burial ground of giants. The setting sun had left a streak of fiery red and then was lost in the thick gloom of darkest night.

"What place is this?" asked Scrooge.

"A place where miners live, who work deep underground," the ghost said. "But they know me. See!"

A light shone from the window of a hut, and they advanced towards it. Passing through the wall of mud and stone, they found a cheerful company assembled round a glowing fire. An old, old man and woman, with their children and their children's children, and another generation beyond that, all decked out gaily in their holiday attire. The old man was singing them a Christmas song that had been very old when he was a boy, and from time to time they all joined in the chorus. As they raised their voices, the old man got quite loud, but as soon as they stopped, he became silent.

The ghost did not linger here, but motioned to Scrooge to follow out to the shore. There stood a solitary lighthouse. Great heaps of seaweed clung to its base, and birds rose and fell about it, like the waves they skimmed.

The two men who watched the light had made a fire. Joining their hands over the rough table at which they sat, they wished each other Merry Christmas.

Again the ghost sped on, until he and Scrooge stood on a ship beside the helmsman at the wheel, the lookout in the bow, the officers who had the watch --- and every man among them hummed a Christmas tune, or had a Christmas thought, or spoke below his breath to his companion of some bygone Christmas Day. And every man on board, waking or sleeping, good or bad, had a kinder word for another on that day than on any day in the year, and shared to some extent in its festivities, and remembered the people he cared for at a distance, and knew that they delighted to remember him.

It was a great surprise to Scrooge, while he saw all of this, to hear a hearty laugh. It was a much greater surprise to Scrooge to recognize it as his own nephew's, and to find himself in a bright, dry, gleaming room, with the ghost standing smiling by his side, and looking at that same nephew with approving affability!

"Ha, ha!" laughed Scrooge's nephew. "Ha, ha, ha!"

If you should happen, by any unlikely chance, to know a man more blessed in a laugh than Scrooge's nephew, all I can say is, I should like to know him too.

There is much disease in our world, but there is nothing so irresistibly contagious as laughter and good humor. When Scrooge's nephew laughed in this way --- holding his sides, rolling his head, and twisting his face into the most extravagant contortions --- his wife laughed as heartily as he. And their assembled friends roared out with them.

"He said that Christmas was a humbug!" cried Scrooge's nephew. "He believed it too!"

"More shame for him, Fred!" his wife said.

"He's a comical old fellow," said Scrooge's nephew. "That's the truth, and not so pleasant as he might be. But his crimes carry their own punishment, and I have nothing to say against him."

"I'm sure he is very rich, Fred," his wife said.

"What of that, my dear!" said Scrooge's nephew. "His wealth is of no use to him. He doesn't do any good with it. He doesn't make himself comfortable with it. He hasn't the satisfaction of thinking -- ha, ha, ha! -- that he is ever going to benefit us with his fortune."

"I have no patience with him," she said, and her sisters and all the other ladies expressed the same opinion.

"Oh, I have!" said Scrooge's nephew. "I am sorry for him; I couldn't be angry with him if I tried. Who suffers by his foul mood? He does, always. Here, he takes it into his head to dislike us, and he won't come and dine with us. What's the consequence? He loses a very good dinner."

Then Scrooge's nephew turned serious: "I mean to invite him to join us every year, whether he likes it or not, for I pity him. He may mock Christmas till he dies, but he can't help thinking better of it if I go there, in good humor, year after year, saying 'Uncle Scrooge, how are you?' If it only puts him in the vein to leave his poor clerk fifty pounds, that's something."

After tea, they had some music. And all the things that the ghost had shown him filled Scrooge's mind. He softened more and more, and thought that if he could have listened to music more often, years ago, he might have cultivated the kindnesses of life for his own happiness.

After a while, Scrooge's nephew and his children played games, and Scrooge saw how it is good to be young sometimes, and never better than at Christmas. There might have been twenty people there, young and old, but they all played, and so did Scrooge, who forgot that his voice made no sound in their ears and sometimes came out, and quite loudly at that, with his guess to their quizzes.

The ghost was pleased to find Scrooge in this mood, and was delighted when Scrooge begged like a boy to be allowed to stay until the guests departed. But the ghost said this could not be done.

"They're starting a new game," said Scrooge. "One half hour, Spirit, only one!"

It was a game called Yes and No, where Scrooge's nephew had to think of something, and the rest must find out what. He only answered their questions yes or no, as the case was. The brisk fire of questioning to which he was exposed produced these responses: He was thinking of an animal, a live animal, rather a disagreeable animal, a savage animal, an animal that growled and grunted sometimes, and talked sometimes, and lived in London, and walked about the streets, but it didn't live in a menagerie, and was never killed in a market, and was not a horse, or an ass, or a cow, or a bull, or a tiger, or a dog, or a pig, or a cat, or a bear.

At every fresh question that was put to him, the nephew burst into a fresh roar of laughter.

At last his sister cried out: "I have it! I know what it is, Fred! I know what it is!"

"What is it?"

"It's your Uncle Scro-o-o-o-oge!"

Which it certainly was. Admiration was the universal sentiment, though some objected that the reply to "Is it a bear?" ought to have been "Yes," because an answer in the negative was sufficient to have diverted their thoughts from Mr. Scrooge.

"He has given us plenty of merriment, I am sure," said Fred, "and it would be ungrateful not to drink his health." He reached for a glass of mulled wine. "To Uncle Scrooge!"

"Well! Uncle Scrooge!" they cried.

"A Merry Christmas and a Happy New Year to the old man, whatever he is!" said

Scrooge's nephew. "He wouldn't take it from me, but may he have it, nevertheless. Uncle Scrooge!"

Uncle Scrooge had imperceptibly become so gay and light of heart that he would have toasted his nephew's family in return if the ghost had given him time. But the whole scene passed with the last word spoken by his nephew, and Scrooge and the ghost were again upon their travels.

Much they saw, and far they went, and many homes they visited, but always with a happy end. The ghost stood by sick beds, and they were cheerful. He showed Scrooge foreign lands, and they seemed close at home. He visited struggling men, and they seemed patient in their greater hope. He went to the poor, and they were rich. In hospitals and jails, in misery's every refuge, the ghost left his blessing and taught Scrooge new lessons.

It was a long night, and a strange one, for while Scrooge remained physically un-changed, the ghost grew older, clearly older. Scrooge had observed this change, but never spoke of it, until they left a children's Twelfth Night party, when he looked at the ghost as they stood together in an open place and noticed that its hair was grey.

"Are spirits' lives so short?" asked Scrooge.

"My life upon this globe, is very brief," replied the ghost. "It ends tonight."

"Tonight!" cried Scrooge.

"Tonight at midnight. Hark! The time is drawing near."

The chimes were ringing the three quarters past eleven at that moment.

"Forgive me," said Scrooge, looking intently at the ghost's robe, "but I see something strange, and not belonging to your, protruding from your robe. Is it a foot... or a claw?"

"It might be a claw, for there is flesh upon it," was the Ghost's sorrowful reply. "Look here."

From his robe, two children appeared. They were wretched, abject, frightful, hideous, miserable. They knelt down at its feet, and clung upon the outside of its garment.

"Look, look, down here!" exclaimed the ghost.

They were a boy and girl. Yellow, ragged, scowling, wolfish --- but also humble.

Scrooge was appalled. Having them shown to him in this way, he tried to say they were fine children, but the words choked themselves.

"Spirit! Are they yours?" was all Scrooge could say.

"They are Man's," said the ghost, looking down upon them. "This boy is Ignorance. This girl is Need. Beware them both."

"Have they no home or help?" cried Scrooge.

"Are there no prisons?" said the ghost, turning on Scrooge for the last time with his own words. "Are there no workhouses?"

The bell struck twelve.

Scrooge looked about him for the ghost, and didn't see it. As the last stroke ceased to vibrate, he remembered the prediction of old Jacob Marley, and lifting up his eyes, he saw a solemn phantom, draped and hooded, coming, like a mist along the ground, towards him.

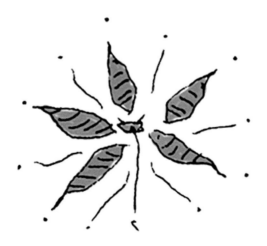

CHAPTER 4
THE LAST OF THE SPIRITS

The phantom approached. Slowly. Silently. It was shrouded in a deep black garment, which concealed its head, its face, its form. It seemed to scatter gloom with every step.

Scrooge, bent down on one knee, could only see an outstretched hand. He felt that it was tall and stately when it came beside him, and that its mysterious presence filled him with a solemn dread.

"You are the ghost of Christmas Yet To Come?" said Scrooge.

The phantom didn't answer, but pointed onward with its hand.

"You are about to show me shadows of the things that have not happened, but will happen in the time before us? Is that so, Spirit?"

The upper portion of the garment moved. That was the only answer he received.

Although he was becoming used to ghostly company, Scrooge feared the silent shape so much that his legs trembled beneath him, and when he prepared to follow the ghost, he could hardly stand.

"Ghost of the Future!" he exclaimed. "I fear you more than any I have seen. But as I know your purpose is to do me good, and as I hope to live to be another man from what I was, I am prepared to go where you lead, and do it with a thankful heart. But please… won't you speak to me?"

The phantom made no reply. It just pointed its hand straight ahead.

"Alright, then," said Scrooge. "Lead on!"

Scrooge followed, and then the phantom's robe circled around him, lifting him up and carrying him along.

Suddenly there were in the heart of the city. Merchants hurried up and down. The phantom stopped beside a group of businessmen. Observing that the hand was pointed to them, Scrooge leaned in to listen to their talk.

"No," said a very fat man with a monstrous chin, "I don't know much about it, either way. I only know he's dead."

"When did he die?"

"Last night, I believe."

"I thought he'd never die --- what was the matter with him?"

"God knows."

"What has he done with his money?" asked a red-faced gentleman.

"I haven't heard," said the man with the large chin. "Left it to his Company, perhaps. He hasn't left it to me. That's all I know."

"It's likely to be a very cheap funeral," another man said. "I mean, I don't know of anybody to go to it. But I don't mind going if a lunch is provided."

They all laughed, and walked on.

Scrooge knew the men, and looked towards the phantom for an explanation.

The phantom led him to the next street, where two other men were talking. Scrooge knew these men. They were men of business: very wealthy, and of great importance. He had always made a point of treating them well --- that is, in a business way of treating someone well.

"How are you?" said one.

"How are you?" said the other.

"Well!" said the first. "Old Scratch has got his own at last, hey?"

"So I am told. Cold, isn't it?"

"Seasonable for Christmas time."

"It is. Good morning!"

Not another word. That was their meeting, their conversation, and their parting.

Scrooge was at first inclined to be surprised that the phantom should attach importance to conversations apparently so trivial. But he was sure they must have some hidden purpose, and he considered what it might be. They could scarcely be supposed to have any bearing on the death of Jacob, his old partner, for that was Past, and this phantom's interest was the Future. And he couldn't think of anyone immediately connected to him to whom these remarks might apply. Still, he resolved to treasure up every word he heard, and everything he saw, and especially to observe the shadow of himself when it appeared. He had an expectation that the conduct of his future self would give him the clue he missed and would help him solve these riddles.

He looked around for his own image; but another man stood in his usual corner. That gave him little surprise, because he had been thinking hard about changing his life, and he thought his absence from these streets meant he had done just that.

They went next into an obscure part of the town, where the streets were dirty, the shops and houses needed paint, and the people were badly dressed and ugly. The neighborhood reeked of poverty and misery.

They came to a shop where iron, old rags and bottles were bought. The floor was covered with piles of rusty keys, nails, chains, hinges, files, scales, weights and scraps of iron. Sitting in the center was a grey-haired rascal, nearly seventy years old.

Just then a woman with a heavy bundle slunk into the shop. She was followed by another woman and a man in faded black. They all seem surprised to be meeting one another there.

The first woman threw her bundle on the floor, looking with bold defiance at the other two.

"Every person has a right to take care of themselves," she said. "He always did!"

"Very true," the other woman said. "Who's the worse for the loss of a few things like these? Not a dead man, I suppose."

"If he wanted to keep 'em after he was dead, why wasn't he nicer when he was alive?" the first woman said. "If he had been, he'd have had somebody to look after him when he was struck by death, instead of lying gasping out his last hours, alone by himself."

"That's the truest word that ever was spoke," the man said. "It's a judgment on him."

"I wish it was a little heavier judgment," replied the woman. She turned to the shop-keeper. "Open that bundle, old Joe, and let me know the value of it."

The others had the same idea, and soon there was a new pile: a pencil-case, a battered watch, sheets and towels, two old-fashioned silver teaspoons, a pair of sugar-tongs, a few boots --- even a blanket.

"His blankets?" Joe asked.

"Whose else's do you think?" replied the woman. "He isn't likely to take cold without them."

Scrooge listened to this dialogue in horror.

"Spirit!" said Scrooge, shuddering from head to foot. "I see, I see. The case of this unhappy man might be my own. My life tends that way now. Merciful Heaven, what is this!"

He recoiled in terror, for the scene had changed, and now he saw a bare bed. Under a ragged sheet, there lay something covered up. Then a pale light fell upon the bed, and on it, unwatched and uncared for, was the body of a man.

The slightest raising of the cover would have revealed the face. Scrooge thought of it, felt how easy it would be to do it, and longed to do it --- but he just could not bring himself to do it.

"Spirit!" he said, "this is a fearful place. In leaving it, I shall not leave its lesson, trust me. Let us go!"

The phantom pointed to the head.

"If there is any person in the town who feels emotion caused by this man's death," said Scrooge, "show that person to me, Spirit, I beseech you!"

The phantom spread its dark robe before him for a moment, like a wing. When he opened it, it seemed to be daylight, and Scrooge was a room with a mother and her children.

She was expecting someone, and she seemed quite anxious, for she walked up and down the room, jerked at every sound, looked out the window, glanced at the clock, and could hardly bear the voices of the children in their play.

At length the long-expected knock was heard. She hurried to the door and met her husband, a man whose face was careworn and depressed, though he was young. There was a remarkable expression in it now, a kind of delight of which he felt ashamed.

He sat down to the dinner that had been waiting for him by the fire.

"Is it good." she said, "or bad?"

"Bad," he answered.

"We are quite ruined?"

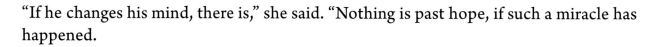

"No. There is hope yet, Caroline."

"If he changes his mind, there is," she said. "Nothing is past hope, if such a miracle has happened.

"He is past changing his mind," her husband said. "He is dead."

She was thankful in her soul to hear it, and she said so, with clasped hands. In the next moment, she said she was sorry and asked for forgiveness, but the first was the emotion of her heart.

"To whom will our debt be transferred?"

"I don't know. But before that time we shall be ready with the money, and even if we aren't, no one would be as hard on us as he was. We may sleep tonight with light hearts, Caroline!"

Yes. Soften it as they would, their hearts were lighter. The children's faces were brighter --- it was a happier house for this man's death! Here, the only emotion that the phantom could show Scrooge was one of pleasure.

"Let me see some tenderness connected with a death," said Scrooge, "or that dark chamber, Spirit, which we left just now, will be forever present to me."

The phantom conducted him through several familiar streets, and as they went along, Scrooge looked here and there to find himself, but nowhere was he to be seen. They entered poor Bob Cratchit's house and found the mother and the children seated round the fire.

Quiet. Very quiet. The noisy little Cratchits were as still as statues in one corner, and sat looking up at Peter, who had a book before him. The mother and her daughters were engaged in sewing. But surely they were very quiet!

"'And he took a child, and set him in the midst of them."

Where had Scrooge heard those words? He had not dreamed them. The boy must have read them out, as he and the phantom crossed the threshold. Why did he not go on?

The mother laid her work upon the table and put her hand to her face.

"The color hurts my eyes," she said.

The color? Ah, poor Tiny Tim!

"They're better now again," said Cratchit's wife. "It makes them weak by candlelight. and I wouldn't show weak eyes to your father when he comes home, which should be soon."

Peter shut his book. "But I think he has walked a little slower than he used to, these few last evenings, mother."

They were very quiet again. At last she said, in a steady, cheerful voice, that only faltered once: "I have known him walk with --- I have known him walk with Tiny Tim

upon his shoulder, very fast indeed."

"And so have I," cried Peter. "Often."

"And so have I!" exclaimed another. So had all.

"But he was very light to carry," she resumed, intent upon her work, "and his father loved him so, that it was no trouble, no trouble. And there is your father at the door!"

She hurried out to meet him, and Bob in his comforter came in. His tea was ready for him, and they all tried to be the one who helped him to it. Then the two young Cratchits got upon his knees and laid a little cheek against his face, as if they were saying, "Don't mind it, father. Don't be sad!"

Bob was very cheerful with them, and spoke pleasantly to all the family. He looked at the work upon the table, and praised the industry and speed of Mrs. Cratchit and the girls. They would be done long before Sunday, he said.

"Sunday! You went today, then, Robert?" said his wife.

"Yes, my dear. I wish you could have gone. It would have done you good to see how green a place it is. But you'll see it often. I promised him that I would walk there on a Sunday. My little, little child! My little child!"

He broke down all at once. He couldn't help it.

He left the room, and went upstairs into the room above, which was lighted cheerfully, and hung with Christmas. There was a chair set close beside the child. Poor Bob sat down in it, and when he had thought a little and composed himself, he kissed the little face and went down again, quite happy now.

They drew about the fire, and talked. Bob told them of the extraordinary kindness of Mr. Scrooge's nephew, whom he barely knew once. They had met in the street that day, and Bob had shared his sad news. "I'm so sorry," Scrooge's nephew had said. He had given Bob his card. "If I can be of service to you in any way, that's where I live. Pray come to me."

"I'm sure he's a good soul!" said Mrs. Cratchit.

"You would be surer of it, my dear," Bob said, "if you saw and spoke to him. I shouldn't be at all surprised, mark what I say, if he got Peter a better situation."

"And then," cried one of the girls, "Peter will be keeping company with someone, and setting up for himself."

"Get along with you!" retorted Peter, grinning.

"It's just as likely as not," said Bob, "There's plenty of time for that, my dear. But however and whenever we part from one another, I am sure we shall none of us forget poor Tiny Tim."

"Never, father!" they all said.

"And I know," said Bob, "I know, my dears, that when we recollect how patient and how mild he was, even though he was a little, little child, we won't quarrel among ourselves and forget poor Tiny Tim in doing it."

"No, never, father!" they all said again.

"I am very happy," Bob said. "I am very happy!"

Mrs. Cratchit kissed him, his daughters kissed him, the two young Cratchits kissed him, and Peter shook his hand.

"Spirit," said Scrooge, "something informs me that our parting moment is at hand. I know it, but I know not how. Tell me what man that was whom we saw lying dead?"

The ghost of Christmas Yet To Come brought Scrooge to rooms where businessmen gather, but he did not see himself. Indeed, the phantom did not stay for anything, but went straight on.

"This is where my business is," said Scrooge, "and this is my house. Let me behold what I shall be in days to come."

The phantom stopped. The hand was pointed elsewhere.

"The house is right there," Scrooge exclaimed. "Why do you point away?"

The finger didn't move.

Scrooge hastened to the window of his office, and looked in. It was an office still, but not his. The furniture was not the same, and he was not the figure in the chair.

The phantom pointed as before.

They reached an iron gate. Scrooge paused to look round before entering.

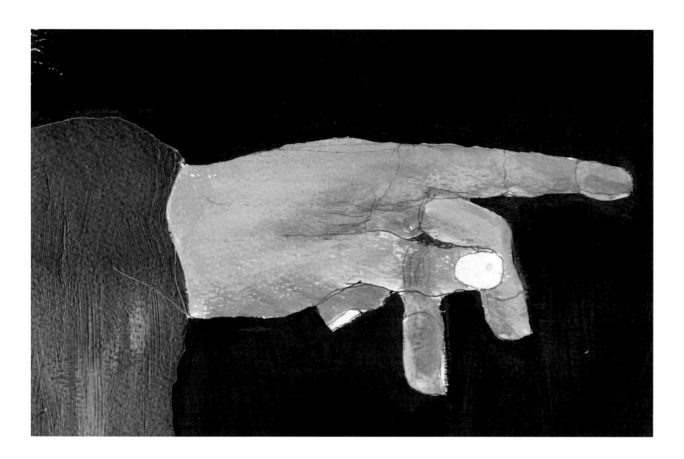

A churchyard. Here, then, the wretched man whose name he had now to learn lay underneath the ground. The phantom stood among the graves, and pointed down to one. Scrooge advanced towards it, trembling.

"Before I draw nearer to that stone to which you point, answer me one question. Are these the shadows of the things that will be, or are they only shadows of things that may be?"

The phantom pointed downward to the grave by which it stood.

"The way men live suggests how they will end," Scrooge said. "But if they change, the ends will change. Say it is thus with what you show me!"

The phantom was immovable as ever.

Scrooge crept towards the grave. And, following the finger, he read upon the stone of the neglected grave his own name: Scrooge.

"Am I that man who lay upon the bed?" he cried.

The finger pointed from the grave to him, and back again.

"No, Spirit! Oh no, no!"

The finger still was there.

"Spirit!" he cried, tightly clutching at its robe. "Hear me! I am not the man I was. I will not be the man I must have been. Why show me this, if I am past all hope?"

For the first time the hand appeared to shake.

"Good Spirit, assure me that I yet may change these shadows you have shown me. Tell me I can change my life!"

Now the hand trembled.

"I will honor Christmas in my heart, and try to keep it all the year," Scrooge said. "I will live in the past, the present, and the future. The spirits of all three shall strive within me. I will not shut out the lessons that they teach. Oh, tell me I may sponge away the writing on this stone!"

In his agony, he caught the phantom's hand. It sought to free itself, but he was strong and held on to it.

And then the phantom shrunk, collapsed, and dwindled down into a bedpost.

PART 5
THE END OF IT

The bed was his own, the room was his own.

Best and happiest of all, the rest of his life was his own --- he had time to make things right!

"I will live in the past, the present, and the future!" Scrooge repeated, as he scrambled out of bed. "The spirits of all three shall strive within me. Oh, Jacob Marley! Oh, Heaven, and Christmas be praised for this! I say it on my knees, old Jacob, on my knees!"

Scrooge's face had been wet with tears. Now he was glowing with his good intentions, and his hands were busy with his clothes --- turning them inside out, putting them on upside down, tearing them, mislaying them.

"I don't know what to do!" he cried. "I am as light as a feather, I am as happy as an angel, I am as merry as a schoolboy. A merry Christmas to everybody! A happy New Year to all the world! Hello, there! Hello!"

He had run into the sitting room, and was now standing there, out of breath.

"There's the door, by which the ghost of Jacob Marley entered!" he all but shouted. "There's the corner where the ghost of Christmas present sat! It's all true, it all happened. Ha ha ha!"

He laughed and laughed --- and for a man who had been out of practice for so many years, it really was a splendid laugh.

"I don't know what day of the month it is," said Scrooge. "I don't know how long I've been among the spirits. I don't know anything. I'm quite a baby. Never mind. I don't care. I'd rather be a baby. Hello! Hello, there!"

Church bells were ringing, the loudest peals he had ever heard. Clash, clang, hammer; ding, dong, bell! Bell, dong, ding, hammer, clang, clash! Oh, glorious, glorious!

Running to the window, he opened it, and put out his head. No fog, no mist. The day was clear, bright, stirring, cold, weather for the blood to dance to. Golden sunlight, heavenly sky, sweet fresh air, merry bells --- oh, glorious! Glorious!

"What's today?" cried Scrooge, calling down to a boy in Sunday clothes.

"Today?" replied the boy. "Why, Christmas Day."

"Christmas Day --- I haven't missed it. The spirits have done it all in one night. They can do anything they like. Of course they can. Of course they can." He leaned out again and called to the boy: "Do you know the butcher in the next street?"

"I should hope I do."

"An intelligent boy!" Scrooge said. "A remarkable boy! Do you know whether they've sold the prize turkey that was hanging up there? Not the little prize turkey --- the big one?"

"What, the one as big as me?"

"What a delightful boy! It's a pleasure to talk to him. Yes, that one!"

"It's hanging there now."

"Go and buy it. And tell them to bring it here, so I can tell them where to take it. Come back with the man, and I'll give you a tip. Come back with him in less than five minutes and I'll double it."

The boy was off like a shot.

"I'll send it to Bob Cratchit," Scrooge whispered, rubbing his hands. "But he won't know who sends it."

The hand in which he wrote the address was not a steady one, but write it he did, somehow, and went downstairs to open the door --- he was that eager to be ready for the coming of the butcher's man.

As he stood there, waiting his arrival, the knocker caught his eye.

"I shall love it, as long as I live!" cried Scrooge, patting it with his hand. "I scarcely ever looked at it before. What an honest expression it has in its face. It's a wonderful knocker. Oh, here's the turkey. Hello! How are you? Merry Christmas!"

It was quite a turkey! He never could have stood upon his legs, that bird. They would have snapped off in a minute. So he added more money, and sent it on in a cab.

Scrooge dressed in his best suit, and at last went out into the streets. The people were by this time pouring forth, as he had seen them with the ghost of Christmas Present. Walking with his hands behind him, Scrooge regarded everyone with a delighted smile. He looked so pleasant that three or four men said, "Good morning, sir! A merry Christmas to you!" And Scrooge said often afterwards, that of all the sounds he had ever heard, those were the sweetest in his ears.

He had not gone far when he saw the man who had walked into his office just the day before and said, "Scrooge and Marley's, I believe." It sent a pang across his heart to think how this old gentleman would look upon him when they met; but he knew what path lay straight before him, and he took it.

"My dear sir," said Scrooge, quickening his pace and taking the old gentleman by both his hands. "How do you do? I hope you succeeded yesterday. It was very kind of you. A merry Christmas to you, sir!"

"Mr. Scrooge?"

"Yes. That is my name, and I fear it may not be pleasant to you. Allow me to ask your pardon. And will you have the goodness" --- here Scrooge whispered in his ear.

"Lord bless me!" cried the gentleman, as if his breath were taken away. "My dear Mr. Scrooge, are you serious?"

"If you please," said Scrooge. "Not a penny less. A great many back payments are included in it, I assure you."

"My dear sir," said the man, shaking hands with him. "I don't know what to say to such generosity…"

"Don't say anything, please," replied Scrooge. "Come and see me. Will you come and see me?"

"I will!" cried the old gentleman. And it was clear he meant to do it.

He went to church, and walked about the streets, and patted children on the head, and questioned beggars, and looked down into the kitchens of houses, and up to the windows, and found that everything could yield him pleasure. He had never dreamed that any walk --- that anything --- could give him so much happiness.

In the afternoon he turned his steps towards his nephew's house.

He passed the door a dozen times before he had the courage to go up and knock.

"Who's there?" called a voice from within.

"It's Uncle Scrooge. I have come to dinner. Will you let me in?"

Let him in! So they did, and he was at home in five minutes. Nothing could be heartier. Wonderful party, wonderful games, wonderful unanimity, wonderful happiness!

But he was early at the office next morning. Oh, he was early there. If he could only be there first, and catch Bob Cratchit coming late! That was the thing he had set his heart upon.

And he did it; yes, he did! The clock struck nine. No Bob. A quarter past. No Bob. He was full eighteen minutes and a half late. Scrooge sat with his door wide open, that he might see him come in.

Bob's hat was off before he opened the door. He was on his stool in a jiffy, scribbling away with his pen, as if working fast and hard would turn back the clock.

"Hello!" growled Scrooge, in his accustomed voice, as near as he could feign it. "What do you mean by coming here at this time of day?"

"I am very sorry, sir."

"Yes, you are! Step this way, sir, if you please."

"It's only once a year, sir. It shall not be repeated. I was making rather merry yesterday, sir."

"I am not going to stand this sort of thing any longer. And therefore," Scrooge continued, leaping from his stool, "I am about to raise your salary!"

Bob trembled.

"A merry Christmas, Bob!" said Scrooge, with an earnestness that could not be mistaken, as he clapped him on the back. "A merrier Christmas, Bob, my good fellow, than I have given you for many a year! I'll raise your salary, and I'll help your struggling family."

Scrooge was better than his word. He did it all, and infinitely more, and to Tiny Tim, who did not die, he was a second father. He became a good friend. Some people laughed to see the change in him, but he let them laugh, for he was wise enough to know that nothing ever happened for good at which some people did not have their fill of laughter in the beginning.

He had no more visits from ghosts, and it was always said of him, that he knew how to keep Christmas well, if any man alive possessed the knowledge. May that be truly said of us, of all of us!

And so, as Tiny Tim observed, "God Bless Us, Every One!"

THE END

Digital graphics – David M. Gotz
Layout – David M. Gotz and Paige Peterson
Cover design – Janine M. Tusa
Everything else – the incomparable Tina M. Keane

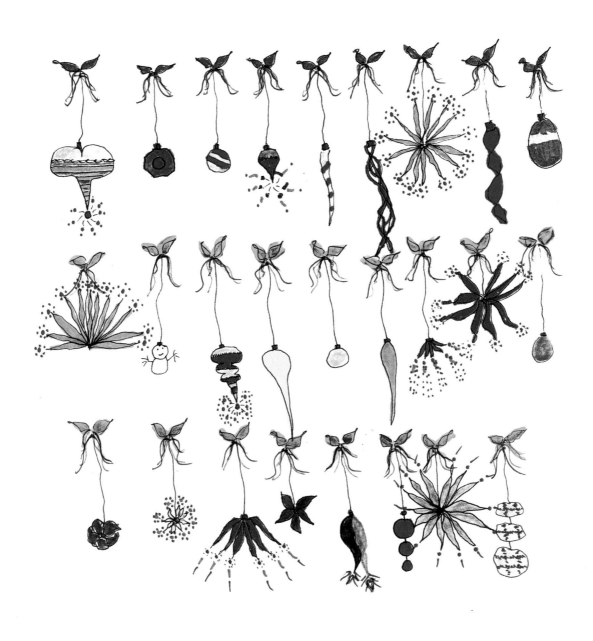

Jesse Kornbluth has been a Contributing Editor of *Vanity Fair* and *New York*, and has written or co-authored a dozen books. He has been Editorial Director of *America Online* and now edits a cultural web site, HeadButler.com. He is the father of one child and lives in New York City.

jessekornbluth.com

Jesse Kornbluth and Paige Peterson   Photo by Peter Cary Peterson

Paige Peterson has had numerous gallery shows in New York and California. The Guild Hall Academy of the Arts in East Hampton has honored her with a lifetime membership. She is the Author and Artist in Residence at Literacy Partners. She is the author of *Growing Up Belvedere-Tiburon* and the co-author and illustrator of *Blackie: The Horse Who Stood Still*. She has two adult children and lives in New York City.

paigempeterson.com